There is no one method or technique that is the ONLY way to learn to read. Children learn in a variety of ways. **Read with me** is an enjoyable and uncomplicated scheme that will give your child reading confidence. Through exciting stories about Kate, Tom and Sam the dog, **Read with me**:

- *teaches the first 300 key words (75% of our everyday language) plus 500 additional words*

- *stimulates a child's language and imagination through humorous, full colour illustration*

- *introduces situations and events children can relate to*

- *encourages and develops conversation and observational skills*

- *support material includes Practice and Play Books, Flash Cards, Book and Cassette Packs*

Always praise and encourage as you go along. Keep your reading sessions short and stop immediately if your child loses interest.

Ladybird books are widely available, but in case of
difficulty may be ordered by post or telephone from:

Ladybird Books – Cash Sales Department
Littlegate Road Paignton Devon TQ3 3BE
Telephone 0803 554761

A catalogue record for this book is available
from the British Library

Published by Ladybird Books Ltd Loughborough Leicestershire UK
Ladybird Books Inc Auburn Maine 04210 USA

Printed in England

Read with me
Sam
to the rescue

by WILLIAM MURRAY
stories by JILL CORBY
illustrated by TERRY BURTON

Tom and Kate are here.

Kate has a toy.

Tom has the ball.

Sam is not here.

Sam looks for
the toy he likes.

The toy is not here.

He looks for the toy.

Here they are.
Here they are in a tree.

Tom, I can jump.
Can you jump like I can?

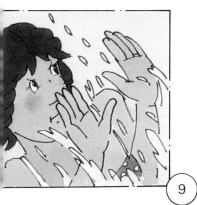

No,
Kate,
no.

Look here, Tom,
look at this.

In here, Tom,
look at this.

He comes and looks.

They look at the fish
in the water.

Sam looks at the
fish in the water.

No, Sam, no,
you can't have it.

It's not for you.

The fish can jump.
It jumps up.

Look at it jump,
says Kate to Tom.

They like to look
at the fish.

Like this,
Tom says to Kate.

It's fun.

Yes, like this,
Kate says to Tom.

We like it.

They are in the shop.

I want a ball, please,
says Tom.

Yes, says Kate.
And I want a boat,
please.

We can have fun,
they say.

Here you are,
says Tom.

We want to have fun.

Look, down comes
the ball.

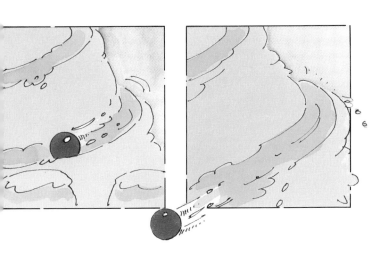

Yes, here it comes,
down, down, he says.

Come here,
Tom and Kate.

Some for you, Kate
and some for you, Tom.

You can't have this,
Sam.

Here is some water
for you.

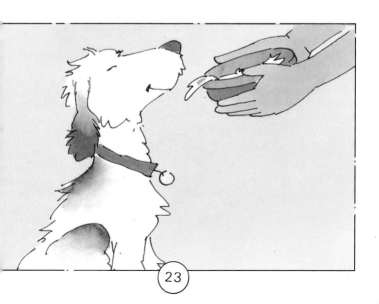

Sam looks for the toy.
He wants it.
He likes the toy.

No, Sam, you can't have it.
It's not a toy.

Here is the boat,
Tom and Kate.

Have a go in it.

Sam can't go
in the boat.

Sam likes to go
into the water.
He jumps in.

Tom says, I want you
to come in, Kate.

No, no, Tom!

Here is Tom's hat.
Look, says Kate,
a fish is in the hat.

The fish in the hat
jumps up.

It jumps into the water.

Have some,
Kate and Tom.

The dog jumps up.
Down, Sam, down.

Yes, Sam,
you can have some.

He can have some,
says Kate.

Look, Tom, look!

Look at this,
says Kate.

Go in the water, please,
Tom says to the dog.

The dog jumps
into the water.

Go for it, Sam,
they say.

Here comes Sam.
He has the boat.

Look at this,
says Tom.

The water has come in,
he says.

And look at this,
says Kate.
Sam, you look at this.

We have to go,
Tom says.
Yes, we have to go,
Kate says.

No, no, Sam,
you can't have it.

Here you are.
Here we go.

Words introduced in this book

Number of words used............................32

These are the same 32 words which were introduced in Book 3. All are Key Words.